The Horror of the Black Light

The Slime Files

Look out for more stories about
Bucket and Delroy!

The Terror of the Fireworms

www.jandean.co.uk

The Horror of the
Black Light

Jan Dean

illustrated by Steve Cox

This edition produced for the Book People Ltd,
Hall Wood Avenue, Haydock, St Helens WA11 9UL

First published by Scholastic Ltd, 2002
This edition published by Scholastic Ltd, 2005

Text copyright © Jan Dean, 2002
Illustrations copyright © Steve Cox, 2002

ISBN 0 439 95561 0

Printed and bound by Nørhaven Paperback A/S, Denmark

Chapter One

Bucket. That's my name – ever since the horrible incident in the supermarket. I can't actually remember the horrible incident, because I was only two when it happened. But my family really like reminding me of it.

Apparently, I was strapped into Mum's trolley when a fluttery lady in a big hat swooped down, gurgling that toddler-speak that grown-ups use on babies.

"Isn't, he a lovely ickle-wickle boy? A lovely-wovely ickle-wickle boy." Then she squished my face like play-dough and burbled, "What's his namey-wamey, then?"

At this point I did three things:

I threw up;

I bit her finger;

I pointed at the "home cleaning" display and said "Bucket!"

That's how I got my nickname. It could have been worse. The next shelf was breakfast cereals – I could have been called Sugar Puff. When you think about it, *Bucket* was a narrow escape.

And it wasn't my only narrow escape. I've been in some tight corners – genuine, blood-run-cold, dangerous stuff. Believe me, I know about narrow escapes...

Last year we moved to Monterey in California. Out in Monterey Bay, under the waves of the Pacific Ocean, is the Monterey Trench – one of the deepest ocean trenches in the world.

"Think *deep*," Dad said. "Now think *deeper – three kilometres* deep. That's the Monterey Trench. And I'm joining the team exploring it." He paused, "Bucket? Are you okay? You look funny."

"His brain is hurting," my sister, Ellen, said. "You know he can't cope with deep thinking."

"Oh, ha ha," I said. "Are you really going undersea exploring?" My dad got seasick in the shower. Could he brave the waves of Monterey Bay? No way.

Dad grinned. "I know what you're thinking."

I hope not, I thought. I was picturing my dad swimming. First, he thrashed about like a man being dragged to his death by a giant squid...

...then *he sank*. And that was in the shallow end.

"You think I've taken secret scuba-diving lessons."

Fat chance, I thought. How could you learn to scuba-dive when you couldn't swim? *Floating* lessons would have been more like it.

"Well, I haven't," he said.

No surprise there, then.

"I won't be going in the water at all," he said. "The Monterey Trench is far too deep for that. All the exploration is done by remote-control probe – and I'll be comfy and dry in the Monterey Aquarium operating it!"

"And we all get to live in California for two years!" Mum said. "Isn't that wonderful?"

And it was. Two years in America. Fantastic.
So we moved to Monterey and I went to
Junior High School and met Delroy, who is
seriously cool and my number one buddy.
He hangs out in the aquarium with me all
the time. And that's where the trouble started.

Delroy likes the sea otters best and that's
where we usually go first. We were on our
way there when we met Dad.

"Hey, Bucket, there are new signals in from
the probe. Want to come and see?"

"Neat," Delroy said.

Dad tapped the access code into the keypad and the security door opened.

"Don't you love that?" Delroy said, as we walked into the private spaces behind the tanks. "Secret codes and passwords – all that stuff. It's like living in a movie."

"I think a movie might smell better," I said as we passed a huge pile of penguin poo cleaned out from the pool.

"Fish smell bad enough, but once they've been through a penguin – boy, do they stink!"

The probe-room was past the penguins and the sea-labs and across a high platform overlooking the ocean. Dad unlocked the door and led us down the steep stairs into the probe-room.

"We should have brought popcorn," Delroy said when he saw the big screen.

"Sit there," Dad said, "and I'll bring the probe on line."

"Wow," Delroy said, politely.

I laughed. "*Wow?*" I looked at the screen. Instead of a smooth black rectangle there was a blurry grey rectangle. It looked like a close-up of the lint from the tumble drier.

"Is that it?" I asked. "Fuzz?"

"Yep," Dad said. "But it is dark and secret fuzz from the mysterious depths of the ocean."

Delroy giggled. The screen cleared. Out of the shadows, a yellow, spidery arm stretched out, then a black, beaky claw inched along beside it.

Delroy gasped. "That's a real spooky fish!"

"No, Delroy, that's the probe," Dad said. "It picks up samples from the sea bed and brings them up for testing."

The screen was fascinating – if you liked mud. And if you liked incredibly ancient and extremely wet mud – it was the most fascinating thing on the planet. Now, I've nothing against mud, but believe me it doesn't make exciting television.

"Okay, Delroy," I said. "Let's go."

But Delroy gazed at the screen. "Hang on, Bucket, something's happening."

A mud cloud was mushrooming up from the sea bed. *Neep. Neep.* The alarm sounded on the computer console. Red lights flashed on the monitor.

"It's got something!"

Through the mud mist we saw the probe holding a globby lump.

"Hey," I said. "It *has* got something. And it looks just like ... wow ... it's incredible... From all that undersea gloop, the probe has picked up a whole bunch of ... MUD."

Delroy gave me a look. "I thought it was kind of exciting. I mean you never know, it might not be mud."

I thought about it. "You're right," I said. "It might be slime."

"But what if it's something *undiscovered*," Delroy insisted. "Like some really freaky life form no one's ever seen before?"

"Delroy — you are the freakiest life form around here. Let's—"

And that's when all the lights went out.

Chapter Two

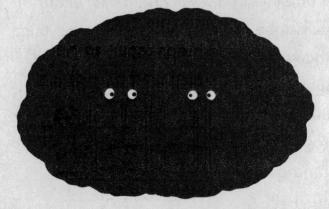

"Don't panic," Dad said, calmly. "Stay put.
I'll feel my way up the stairs and find out
what's happening." Then we heard the door
open and close and we were alone.

In the darkness Delroy whispered, "Bucket?"

"Yeah?"

"Just checking."

"Delroy?"

"Yeah?"

"Why are we whispering?"

"Because it's dark. Everything sounds
louder in the dark."

"Don't be stupid," I said, but then I realized

it was true. Things *do* sound louder in the dark. I was still thinking about this when all the lights came back on – and everything went berserk.

The computer screen flashed up error messages. The fire-bell clanged.

Then, the aquarium's public address system announced: *Danger. Evacuate the building. Danger. Evacuate the building.* We were up the stairs in about ten seconds flat. From the high platform we could hear the chaos. Alarms were sounding off everywhere.

"Crazy," Delroy said, his hands over his ears. "Hey, look!" He was staring out over the water. I looked too.

Whales. The bay was full of them. And more and more surfaced, spouting white fountains of misty breath up into the air.

Then, all at once, they sank under the waves
– as if they'd never been.

"Spooky," Delroy said. "Seriously *spooky*."

"I'm sure there's a reasonable scientific
explanation for it," I said.

"Oh yeah? What?" Delroy said, giving me
a hard stare.

"Well ... maybe the whales set off the alarms,"
I suggested. "Whales make sounds, don't
they? Maybe their singing set off the sensors."

"Give me a break," Delroy sighed. "It's bad enough the aquarium goes mad without you blaming the whales."

"It's not impossible," I insisted.

"Sure it is," Delroy said. "Whales come to Monterey Bay all the time. If they could set off alarms, don't you think they'd have done it before?"

"Well... Okay, then – I give in. It is spooky," I agreed.

It took about an hour to get the place back to normal.

"It's a mystery," Dad said. "No one can work out exactly what went wrong – except that the power cut upset all the computer systems and that's what triggered the alarms. Still – everything's back to normal now."

But it wasn't. The alarms may have been switched off, but the aquarium was *not* normal. We left Dad hard at work and went to the sea-otters. They were huddled together on a rock – absolutely still.

"But they're always clowning around," Delroy said. "Are they sick?"

"Weird," I murmured. "Weird..."

But if we thought that was weird, it was nothing compared with the jellyfish.

The whole lot of them were up against the glass of their tanks, like layers of gloopy wallpaper paste.

"Let's go and find one of the fish-keepers," I said. "Maybe they know why everything's acting crazy."

So we went to the security door and glanced around. We weren't supposed to go back there without Dad, but I'd seen him do the spy-movie keypad-thing a million times. No one was looking, so I tapped in the number and we went behind the scenes.

Chapter Three

The fish in the holding tanks were going bananas. They were in one huge shoal, swimming round, faster and faster, making huge waves that slopped right out of the tanks and crashed on to the floor.

Three fish-keepers were sweeping the water towards the drain, trying to stop the area flooding. We stared at the fish. They swam so fast they were a blur, like a huge silver cylinder spinning in the green water.

"Hey! You kids!" an angry voice called. "How did you get back here?"

A fish-keeper strode towards us, then she recognized us and relaxed. "Oh, it's you, Bucket. Where's your Dad?"

"Umm..." I mumbled.

Delroy got us off the hook. "Can we help?" he asked.

"Grab a broom and start sweeping," she said.

Sweeping water sounds like fun, but it isn't. Fish-tank water stinks. Sweeping fish-water is only one step up from carrying buckets of penguin poo.

"Okay, emergency's over," the fish-keeper said. "You can quit now. Here," she handed us five dollars, "go buy yourselves milkshakes."

"Thanks," Delroy said. "Erm ... we were just wondering—" he began.

"If you knew what had spooked the fish?" I finished.

The keeper shook her head. "It's a mystery," she said. "I'm just glad they've all settled down."

So, no wiser, but wetter and tireder, we went to the cafe.

"We've earned this milkshake," I said to Delroy as I sat down to drink my malted banana special. I was taking my second slurp when Dad arrived.

"Typical," he said. "Everyone in the place has been working their socks off – and here you are drinking milkshakes!"

"But we've — "

"Not now," Dad said. "It's almost five. I promised Mum we'd be home early."

"But my shake..."

"Come on, Bucket."

"My mom's not picking me up until five thirty." Delroy said. "Don't worry, Bucket, I'll finish your shake."

"Oh thanks, Delroy," I said. "I'm overwhelmed."

"Don't mention it," he grinned.

There's no justice. I did all that sweeping, and what did I have to show for it? A blister on my hand and wet feet.

Chapter Four

Next morning, Dad shook me awake.

"C'mon, Bucket, rise and shine!"

I glanced at the clock. Five thirty! "Oh, give me a break," I groaned.

"*Hurry up*, Bucket. Delroy's here."

That woke me. Delroy was allergic to mornings. You could drag him out of bed and hose him down with iced water and he'd still be snoring. Delroy could out-sleep the undead. So why was he at my house at five thirty in the morning?

"Because I called him," Dad grinned. "Delroy's dad works early shifts – he's always up at dawn – I knew there'd be someone to answer the phone."

"But *why*?" I said. Had the world gone nuts? "Why would you call Delroy at dawn?"

"Earthquake," Dad said. "Well, *sea*-quake. Rumblings at the bottom of the trench. Also, we're going to run tests on that *interesting rock* the probe found. I thought you guys could come and see before school."

I gave in. I got dressed, grabbed a glass of OJ from the fridge and gave Delroy a look. I was up at dawn because of a tank full of water with an *interesting* rock in it. Oh wow! What a thrill...

I was so excited I almost fell right back asleep.

"It'll be cool," Delroy said, as Dad drove us downtown.

"No, Delroy," I said. "It won't."

But I was wrong. The scientists in the quake-room were all hyped-up — waving their arms about, flapping papers around, shouting out to each other.

"Something's sure rattled their cage," Delroy said. "That quake must've been something special."

As we watched, the computers buzzed into overdrive and the printers started churning out data. Tonnes of it. Great ribbons of paper rippled out of the machines and all the time the needles charting the sea-quake jerked back and forth like crazy spiders.

"It's opening!" someone shouted.

"The crack in the trench is opening!"

My stomach lurched.

"If something as deep as the Monterey Trench has an even deeper crack in it," I whispered, "maybe the whole world could split in half like an apple."

Delroy gave me a puzzled look. "You know what?" he said. "Maybe you should give your brain a rest..."

Chapter Five

After the frenzy of the quake-room the probe-room was dead calm. Especially when Dad left to get more paper for the printer. Then it was more than calm – it was totally boring.

We peered into the tank at the *interesting rock*. I ask you – who in their right mind puts the word *interesting* next to the word *rock*? The seriously sad – that's who.

"My dad needs new brains," I said. "He got us up at five thirty for this!"

"Well," Delroy hesitated. "It is from the bottom of the ocean."

"It's a rock in water, " I exploded. "It looks like an exhibit they forgot to put the fish in!"

"Yeah, why's it in a tank?" Delroy asked. "Do they think it'll be the first rock in history to make a run for it?"

"It's a pressure tank," I said. "Stuff from the bottom of the sea is built to be super-strong. If the weight of the whole ocean is sitting on top of you, you have to have all this energy inside you pushing outwards, just to keep the ocean from squashing you flat. Take away the pressure and what have you got? All that energy pushing *outwards*, but with nothing pushing it back. An energy bomb. Deep-sea fish just blow up if you don't keep them under pressure."

"Fish-bombs," Delroy muttered. "Gross."
Then he made a funny little choking noise
and jabbed his finger at the tank.

"You okay?"

"Look!"

I looked. Tank. Water. Rock. *Fascinating*...

Then the rock throbbed slightly. Then it
rippled ... and shivered.

"Dad!" I shouted. "Did you see that?"
I glanced towards him. He had just come
back into the room and was staring at the
tank, like me and Delroy. He must have seen
it. Except he hadn't...

I don't know whether grown-ups just *don't see* things, or whether they blank out the evidence of their own eyes. Maybe they just get taken over by ideas. They believe rocks don't wriggle, so when they see a rock wriggling their brains just won't accept it.

"But, Dad," I insisted. "It did. It *wriggled.*"

"Don't be stupid, Bucket," Dad said firmly. "It's a rock. What is it with you two? Did getting up early disturb the delicate balance of your brains? Come on, we'll call in at the drive thru' and have burgers for breakfast. Then I'll get you to school."

Chapter Six

School was not good. By ten o'clock I was outside the principal's office waiting for punishment lecture number one: *Inattention in Mrs Kravitz's Class.* I'd heard it before. It went roughly like this – if you don't pay attention to Mrs Kravitz:

you'll fail your tests,

you won't get to college,

you'll be a total loser and your life won't be worth living.

As far as I could see, life in Mrs Kravitz's class wasn't worth living anyway, so at least I'd be prepared for what was to come.

Right at the end of her lecture, the principal added a new point: "And if you don't pass Mrs Kravitz's term-test, you'll have to do her class all over again next year!" she said.

My blood ran cold. Re-do Krusher Kravitz's class? Aaargh! I went back to class a sadder and a wiser kid. The memory of the rock still nagged me, but I didn't let it distract me from Krusher Kravitz's worksheet. So what if the trench was quaking and throwing up wriggling rocks? The thought of creatures from the trench might give me nightmares, but *a whole extra year with Krusher*? Now **that** was scary!

I met Delroy at lunch. He'd had a bad morning too.

"All I can think about is that rock," he said. "Every class has been a disaster. Mr Benny's put me on report and I have to retake my English test."

"Easy-peasy," I said "I might have to re-do my year with Krusher."

"Double Krusher?" he gasped. "Oh, man!"

We dragged through the afternoon, like prisoners on a chain-gang, but at last the bell rang and we were free.

"Aquarium?" Delroy asked.

"Where else?"

We intended to go straight to the probe-room, but we soon changed our minds.

"Hey, look at the crazy people," Delroy said.

A bunch of visitors were running from tank to tank, pointing at the fish.

"Delroy," I said, slowly, "this is an aquarium – that's what people do."

"Look again, goof!" Delroy said. "That's not normal pointing and shouting. That's *weird* pointing and shouting."

He was right. Looking at fish usually slowed people down. Aquarium visitors were calm. This crowd was manic.

"Let's see what's going on," I said.

The fish were dancing. A tankful of yellow-fin tuna swam into a swirling ball, then fell still. Next, they shot outwards, like a gigantic glass ball splintering to the four corners of the tank. "Wow," Delroy sighed. "Synchronized swimming…"

The tuna were nothing compared with the jellyfish.

The best jellyfish are tiny with little lights running in lines up the side of their umbrella-dome bodies. A jellyfish with lights is like a cross between a plastic bag of milky soup and the Christmas Fairy. Watch them drifting through the blue water and you realize that there are already aliens on planet earth – and that they live in the oceans. I mean, they are so *strange*. And today they were even stranger.

"Is it me?" I asked. "Or are they bigger?"

Delroy gulped. "*Bigger* doesn't quite do it, Bucket. Yesterday they were the size of grapes. Today they're melons. If they carry on at this rate they'll be the size of blue whales by the weekend."

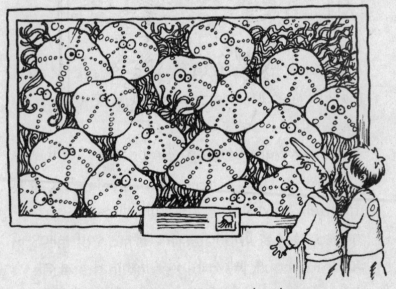

"I think they're going to need a larger tank," I said. "What's doing this stuff? And what's going to happen next?"

Chapter Seven

We made for the probe-room. As we passed the quake-room we saw a huge new map on the wall.

"It's the fault," Delroy said.

"Whose fault?" I said defensively. "It's not my fault."

"No, dope. *The* fault. It's a map of the San Andreas Fault. It's a big crack in the earth that runs under San Francisco. It's why they have earthquakes there."

"I knew that," I said.

There was an undersea map of the trench too, with lots of little red flags marking the line of the new crack. As we watched, a scientist put a whole new row of them in place.

"Boy, that crack is growing fast," I muttered.

"Come on, you kids. Go away now. Your dad's not around and we've no time to babysit," the scientist said.

Don't you hate it when that happens? We weren't doing anything. We weren't in the way. We weren't even asking questions.

"C'mon, Delroy" I said. "Let's go see the rock."

"Sit down and don't mess with anything," Dad said as we opened the probe-room door. "I have to go to the main desk to meet someone from the San Francisco Earthquake Centre."

"Why?"

"It's about our undersea quake. They think it may set off other tremors, so we're on alert – just in case..."

"Is that why the fish are upset?" Delroy asked. "Because of the quake?"

"That's a good question," Dad said. "Things are certainly strange around here, but to be honest, nobody knows why. No one's ever seen anything like it before. Birds and dogs do weird stuff before earthquakes. Maybe fish go bananas before sea-quakes. Who knows? Look – I'll be back as soon as I can. And remember, *don't mess with anything.*"

"It's dark in there, isn't it?" Delroy said as he peered into the pressure tank where the *interesting rock* was.

"This'll help," I said and switched on the aqua-lamps in the tank.

What happened next was mega-weird – and complicated. It went something like this:

1. The lights flickered on and the tank glowed a brighter shade of murky green.

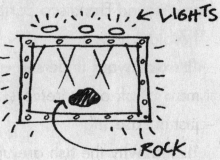

← LIGHTS

ROCK

TANK GOES DARK

2. The very bottom of the tank suddenly went dark, as if someone had poured a whole lot of black ink in it.

3. The inky darkness made itself into a kind of wave and rippled up through the water towards the aqua-lamps.

DARKNESS RIPPLES TOWARDS LIGHT

4. As the dark wave reached the lamps they glowed brighter — amazingly bright — but (and this is the weirdest part of all) although the lamps burned like stars, the tank stayed dark! The black wave just swallowed it like a black sponge soaking up dazzling green paint.

LIGHTS GLOW-BRIGHTER!

TANK GOES DARK!

5. Then the black wave sank to the bottom again, and the lamplight spread through the water like it usually did. For a second it glowed extra bright around the rock — like a green halo — then it was gone and the tank was perfectly normal again.

GLOW AROUND ROCK

"Rocks can't *suck* light, can they?" Delroy asked.

"No," I said.

"They can't *swallow* light, either, can they?"

"Absolutely not," I said firmly.

"So what did we just see?" Delroy asked.

This was a good question – and one that I never had to answer, because at that moment the rock began to move.

"Tell me I'm not seeing that," Delroy said as the rock unfolded itself.

For a second it looked like a writhing nest of worms, then, from the wriggling centre a blunt  jaw emerged. We took a step back.

The creature continued to unfold.

"If it gets much bigger it'll need a new tank by tea-time," I murmured.

A long, crab-like claw reached out and tapped on the glass. Then, quick as a whip, it flicked across the tank and flattened its mouth against the glass. There was a rattling sound, like gravel thrown at a window. Its mouth was full of teeth ... row upon row of razory, glinting teeth, all the way down its throat... We took another step back.

"It's an eating-machine," I gasped. "Those teeth are like the blades in a blender. If that thing got you – you'd be soup!"

We would have taken another step back at this point, but by then we were pressed up against the back wall. There was nowhere else to go. The creature gazed at us with all four of its jelly-slime eyes.

"Do you think it's hungry, Delroy?"

"Ravenous," he whispered, as it opened its mouth and unhinged its jaw like a snake. "Is that glass bite-proof?"

"Well ... tank glass is way thicker than you think," I said.

"So there's nothing to worry about, then?"

"Not a thing," I whispered. "But now would be a good time to turn to butter... Just spread yourself along the wall, Delroy, and melt over to the door. Let's get out of here."

Chapter Eight

We darted up the stairs and on to the platform.
I took a huge gulp of air, then slowly let it out.
I thought of the creature and its zillions of
teeth. "Isn't breathing wonderful?" I sighed.

"Yeah," Delroy agreed. "I really like not
being lunch."

"What are you doing up here?" Dad asked
as he came back from his meeting with the
earthquake man. "I thought you couldn't
stand the smell of penguin poo."

Delroy and I grinned at each other as we took huge deep breaths.

"Penguin poo?" Delroy laughed. "it's perfume to my nose buds."

"Your what?" Dad laughed. And I had to explain to Delroy that although tongues had taste buds, you didn't smell through *nose buds*.

"Who cares?" Delroy said.

"Yeah, right," I nodded. After what we'd just been through, what were a couple of nose buds between friends?

Once we'd told Dad that the rock had turned into a monster-fish he went into overdrive. We tried to tell him about the rock and the strange black light, but we always got the same reply: "Not now, Bucket — can't you see how busy I am?" Every fish-keeper in the aquarium wanted to see the creature. They were practically queuing round the block to get a look at its nasty teeth and its mean eyes.

Dad's precious probe-room had become the big attraction and he was making the most of it. And all the fuss went on for so long that we were really, *really* late getting home.

"How come you're only late when it's *your* turn to cook supper?" Mum asked.

"I'm sorry," Dad said. "Tell you what – let's go into town and have supper on the pier."

Mum gave him a look, but Ellen cheered. She loves the cafes on the pier, where you're only centimetres from the ocean and can watch the sea-otters while you eat.

In our favourite cafe we watched a line of shrimp-boats sail across the bay, their lights twinkling in the dusk.

"You're supposed to cook," Mum said to Dad, "This is nice, but it's cheating."

"It's a mercy mission," I said, "to save us from Dad's sausage and banana casserole."

"Or whatever weird food experiment Dad had planned," Ellen agreed.

"I think sausages and bananas go well together," Dad protested.

"Only in a shape-sorter, dear," Mum said.

Dad's reply was drowned by a thunderclap and a deafening crack of lightning. The whole cafe was lit by vivid blue light, then a great beam, like a black laser, shot up from the ocean into the evening sky.

It moved in a slow arc across the sunset, before swinging abruptly down and reaching towards the shore like a great black arm. It fell across the line of shrimp boats and they disappeared into the darkness. Then the black arm pulsed and grew longer and fatter. It touched the edge of the town and then the lights of Monterey began to go out.

"What on earth...?" Dad stared.

"Is it a power cut?" Mum asked.

"No," I said, "it's black light. It's eating up the energy."

Dad gave me a really odd stare. "Why do you think that?"

"Because I've seen it before," I mumbled. "The rock-thing did it. It kind of sucked up the light in its tank, then it grew..."

Everyone went quiet. If the rock thing could make a small beam of black light, how big was the thing making this massive beam that had just sucked all the electricity out of Monterey...?

"I feel like a milkshake," I said.

Dad stared at me. "Bucket, are you mad? There's a giant energy-eating *thing* out there – and you *want a milkshake*?"

"No. I *feel like* a milkshake – like the last bit in the glass when the straw is slurping up the dregs. Any minute now it'll be *shlupp ... burp ... and bye-bye, Bucket...*"

Then Ellen gasped. "Wow! Look at that!" Once again, the dark beam pointed up at the stars. And around its dense blackness, the most amazing light show was playing...

Golden sparks and blue flashes danced and throbbed around it. Then, like a million bugs made out of electricity, all this sparkling energy ran up the black arm and clumped together at the top like a shining ball of hot electric power. It was like a colossal black "i" with a wild, fiery dot.

As we gazed, the beam opened and *swallowed* the ball of light, like a snake swallowing an egg. Then it disappeared back into the sea, moving so fast it was a black blur.

"I've got to get to the lab," Dad said.
"Bucket – you come with me."

The car wouldn't start. Nobody's car would start. Every battery in Monterey was drained. So we walked. Mum and Ellen set off for home and we went downtown. Everywhere was in darkness, only the stars lit our way. As we reached the aquarium a shadow in the doorway stirred and moved towards us.

Chapter Nine

"Delroy, what are you doing here?"

"The same as you," Delroy said. "As soon as the lights went out I knew – it's that rock-thing, isn't it? It's eating the electricity, like it did in the tank."

"How come everybody knows about this but me?" Dad said.

"*Not now, Bucket – can't you see how busy I am?*" I said. "Sound familiar?"

"But it was *important,*" Dad fumed. "You should have *made* me listen."

"Oh, yeah, right," I said. *Make* him listen? Like, what planet is he actually on?

Delroy changed the subject. "I brought this," he said, waving a torch at us. It's the kind you wind up to recharge the battery."

"Okay, then," Dad said. "Here we go."

The aquarium was spooky in the dark. We crossed the main hall, listening to the tanks bubble and glug. Using Delroy's torch, we could see that the fish were still acting crazy and the otters were squealing – a weird noise, like a zillion squeaky marker-pens sliding down a whiteboard.

"Ouch," Delroy whispered. "That's hard on the ears."

We hurried to the lab. Dad unlocked the door and it swung open. Inside the black room the tanks gurgled. We stared into the blackness. Dad glanced at Delroy. "You know, I think more torches would be good. There's some in the quake-room cupboard. Wait here while I bring a couple."

Delroy nodded towards the open door. "Shall we go in?" he asked.

"It's pitch black, and there's a thing in there that makes a shark look like a cuddly toy. Do you really want to go in?" I said.

Delroy paused. "Well, if it was going to escape and munch its way through the aquarium, it would have done it by now."

So we left the door open to let the moonlight into the room, and went down the stairs.

"It's not so bad," I whispered. "More dark grey than totally black."

I sounded brave, but I didn't feel it. You know that feeling you get down the back of your neck? That *someone-is-watching-me* feeling? Well, I had that feeling from my eyebrows to my toenails. And I knew that the thing watching us had more teeth than a tyrannosaurus. I shivered.

"Don't panic," Delroy whispered. "if we can't see *it, it* can't see us."

"It's from way down deep," I murmured. "It's at home in the dark. You never know..."

"Aw, c'mon, Bucket, I got scared the other day, but I'm over it. We're out here and it's in there – what's to worry about?" And he whizzed the wind-up handle on his torch and

 shone a beam of light across the room into the tank. Big mistake. It was staring at us – with all four jelly eyes.

Delroy's torch lit the murk inside the tank and, just like before, the light had a strange effect on the creature. First of all its skin went dark – as if it were getting a really deep tan right before our eyes. Then the darkness kind of *slid off* its skin and became a dark wave in the water – an inky clot of black light that moved towards the torch beam.

"It's okay, it's okay," Delroy repeated. "It can't get out ... it can't get out..."

Well, maybe *it* couldn't, but light can move through glass – even black light. The beam of darkness moved through the green water, through the thick grey glass and along the flickering torch beam.

Like a snake, the black beam gulped the torchlight, then it continued to search for food. It swerved towards the doorway, and the pearly greyness of the moonlight. Delroy whizzed round the handle of his wind-up torch until it shone again. At once the black light returned to Delroy – sucking up the light – but then it moved beyond the torch and up Delroy's hand and arm. Delroy tried to twist away, but the beam held him fast.

"Hey!" he gasped. "I can't move my fingers. It's sucking all the feeling out of my arm!"

The black light wound around him like a tentacle and he flopped to the floor like a rag-doll, gasping for breath.

Chapter Ten

Delroy was my best friend. I couldn't just stand there, so...

"Bonsai!" I screamed.

I thought I was shouting out the terrifying battle yell of fearless Japanese warriors, but actually that's *"Banzai"* – Bonsai are miniature trees... So, sounding like a lunatic in a garden centre, I went into action.

I ran at the tank and thumped the glass.

The creature swung one eye in my direction, but it kept the other three on Delroy. I didn't have long. Any second now Delroy would be squeezed out like a juiced orange – and I'd be next.

I had to stop it. I felt along the top of the tank, until my fingers touched the pressure seal. I turned it. The lid flipped up with a huge hiss – as if I'd just opened the world's biggest can of cola. In the greyness I saw the black light waver. Then the creature in the tank swelled up. It was like a giant fish balloon, its slimy sides pressing against the sides of the tank, its tentacles uncoiling like huge strings of blubber. It was out of control, bubbling over the top of its tank; getting bigger and bigger like a pan of popcorn gone crazy. Then suddenly there was a sickening, slimy noise and the creature was everywhere. Well, bits of it were.

Scuzzy black slime dripped from the ceiling. A large blob landed on Delroy.

As he came round, he felt the slime on his face. "Oh gross! What have you done to me?"

"Nothing much," I said. "Just saved your life – that's all!

"Oh sure," Delroy said. "What did you do, give me a goo transfusion?"

Typical, I thought. I'm a hero and no one notices. The next time I save someone's life, I'm going to make sure they are awake and watching every moment of it!

"It's okay – no need to thank me," I said. "Exploding a slime monster is no big deal. I do it all the time."

"But *how* did you explode it?" Delroy asked. "Where'd you get the dynamite?"

So I reminded him that if you're a thing from the deep sea, you have all this energy pushing outwards, just to keep the ocean from squashing you flat. "When I broke the seal on the tank," I said, "I released the pressure and the rock-thing exploded, just like an energy bomb. BOOM. Splat. Dribble-dribble. Drip. Yuk."

"Okay, boys," Dad said, shining his torch in my face. "The electricity crisis is over. The power will be back on in about two seconds."

Sure enough, the lights flickered back on, and as they did we saw just how horrible a mess the probe-room was.

"What the—?!"

"Chill, Dad, chill," I said. "I can explain..."

Dad listened, then he asked. "What are all these little pointy bits of gravel?"

"Um, I think they may be teeth," Delroy said quietly, as we half-crunched, half-slid our way across the floor towards the computer which controlled the probe.

"But there are hundreds of them!"

"Teeth!" I said. "That thing could bite you even without teeth." In some ways its teeth were the least scary thing about it – at least teeth were normal. You knew where you were with teeth, but the black light was something else. It could just come out of the ocean and suck the life out of us – any time it liked.

Dad peered at the screen. "There they are," he muttered.

"What?"

"Creatures ... pouring up through the crack in the trench. They're making the black light. It's not one huge creature, it's millions of little ones, acting together to drink up energy from wherever they can."

That's when I had my BIG IDEA.

"Are you okay?" Delroy asked. "Your face has gone kind of funny."

"I'm thinking," I said.

"Yeah," he nodded. "I knew it was something painful."

"Ha ha," I said. "Oh, I do love humour." Then I told them my idea.

"Genius, or what?" I said.

"Let's not get carried away," Dad said. "On the other hand ... it might just work."

So Dad began making phone calls and sending emails and doing all that stuff you need to do to get the whole state of California ready to fight off an invasion from the sea-bed. There was a big meeting in the aquarium. Everyone was involved – the police, coastguard, firemen, even the army.

Dad stood at the front with a flip chart and explained the plan. *My plan.* Once everything was ready, all we could do was wait … and watch.

Chapter Eleven

The best place to watch the bay was the platform above the probe-room, so Dad set up headquarters there. The coastguard set up an emergency radar station and the army set up a field radio. There were so many aerials that the platform began to look like a giant hedgehog. Day and night we watched the sea, waiting. Three days later, just before sunset, the black light came, stabbing the sky like an evil finger.

"This is it," Dad yelled into the radio transmitter. "Get ready to cut off the power."

Slowly the black beam began to probe the shore, sucking the light from the cafes and shops on the pier, then stretching inland towards the homes of Monterey.

"...five ... four ... three ... two ... one... Throw the switch!"

Suddenly the town went dark. Every light everywhere went out. The power had been turned off. In the blue dusk the black beam hesitated. Then it began to sweep the bay, hungry for energy. It reared up from the water, taller and taller against the sky.

"Dad," I whispered nervously, "I know it's a bit late to mention this, but what if it does what the rock-thing did to Delroy? What if it starts on the people now that the electricity's gone?"

"The rock-creature could see Delroy," Dad said. "Whatever's making that beam is down deep in the ocean. If it wants to catch us, it'll have to see us and if it wants to see us, it'll have to come a whole lot closer. And then..."

Suddenly the ocean began to heave. The waves curved into one huge swell, like the dome of a humongous bubble. I thought of the trench creature and its jelly eyes and I imagined a million of them.

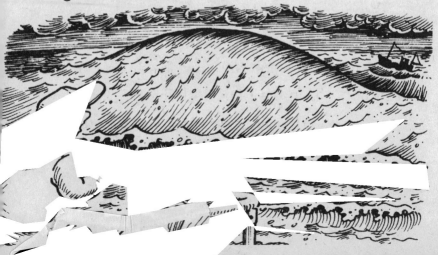

They're coming, I thought, *the monsters from the trench … they're coming!*

All around the rising dome the sea boiled and churned. *A million frogspawn eyes*, I thought, *All staring right at me!*

Just then the explosions began. The whole dome burst into fountains of dark slime. Exploding trench creatures shot into the air like rocket-fish. Slime-bombs splattered everywhere. Fish guts spouted up through the water like party poppers.

The black light rippled and shimmered and then, with a noise like the sky ripping in two, it was gone.

My plan had worked. When we cut off the power, we forced the creatures to come to the surface in search of food. Up here, where the pressure was less – KAPOW – it was "bye-bye trench creatures", "hello Monterey Goo-Fest".

Delroy was impressed. "Every boat in the harbour is totally slimed, and the beach – well, that's just a fish-gut gross-out..."

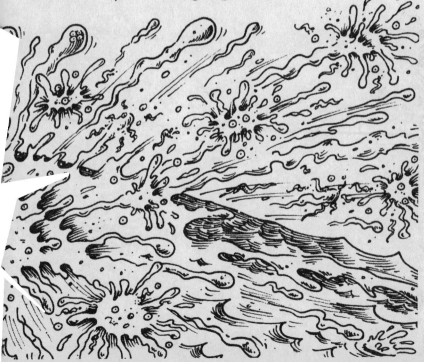

"Messy," I muttered, "but a small price to pay for saving the world..."

Delroy laughed. "Yo, the *Super-Bucket*!"

But our problems weren't over.

"Look out!" Dad shouted. A mega-wave was headed our way.

It hit the beach like liquid thunder, smashing ashore and splintering small boats like matchsticks.

"Something's happening in the trench," Dad said. "Something huge."

The storm raged all night, but by morning
it was calm.

"Well, the Earthquake Centre was right,"
Dad said. "There was another tremor – that's
what caused the giant wave."

I gulped. Another quake. That picture of
the world splitting like an apple jumped back
into my head.

"But this time," Dad continued, "it's *closed*
the crack in the trench."

"Shame," I grinned. "Just as I was getting
used to dealing with slime creatures from the
unknown..."

"Oh, that reminds me," Dad said. "Mum's on the warpath about your room. Something about life forms under your bed..."

I've said it before and I'll say it again – there's no justice. I was *grounded* for leaving a couple of sandwiches under my sports' kit. I ask you, what's a couple of sandwiches compared to saving the world? Even if they were green furry sandwiches with grey stuff oozing out of them... I've seen worse. In fact, I've almost been eaten by worse. Parents! Who needs 'em?